Who Will Play With Me?

For Anna Bootle

Text and illustrations copyright © Michele Coxon, 1992

The moral right of the author/illustrator has been asserted

First published in Great Britain 1992 by Blackie Children's Books

This edition first published 1995 by Happy Cat Books, Bradfield, Essex CO11 2UT

All rights reserved

A CIP catalogue record for this book is available from the British Library

ISBN 1 899248 05 6

Printed in Hong Kong

Who Will Play With Me?

Michele Coxon

Happy Cat Books

Luke had a lovely home.
He had a warm soft bed and plenty of toys.
But he was lonely.
'Who will play with me?'

'Will you play with me?'
'No,' yawned Ben, the old dog.
'I want to sleep and dream of bones.'

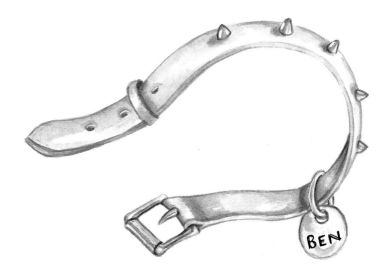

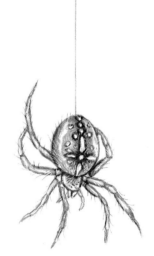

'Will you play with me?'
Luke asked his mum.
'No!' she cried.
'I'm busy, go outside and play.'

'Will you play with me?'
the boy asked a frog.
'No,' croaked the frog.
'I must find some food to eat.'
and he hopped off leaving only a wet puddle.

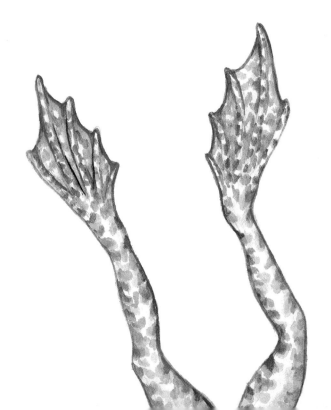

Luke crawled through the jungle of the grass

and came nose to whiskers with a funny creature.
It had two big green eyes, a pink nose and a furry face.

'Will you play with me?'

Turn the page and see who will play with Luke.
Then close the book, turn it upside-down, and start
again from the other end!

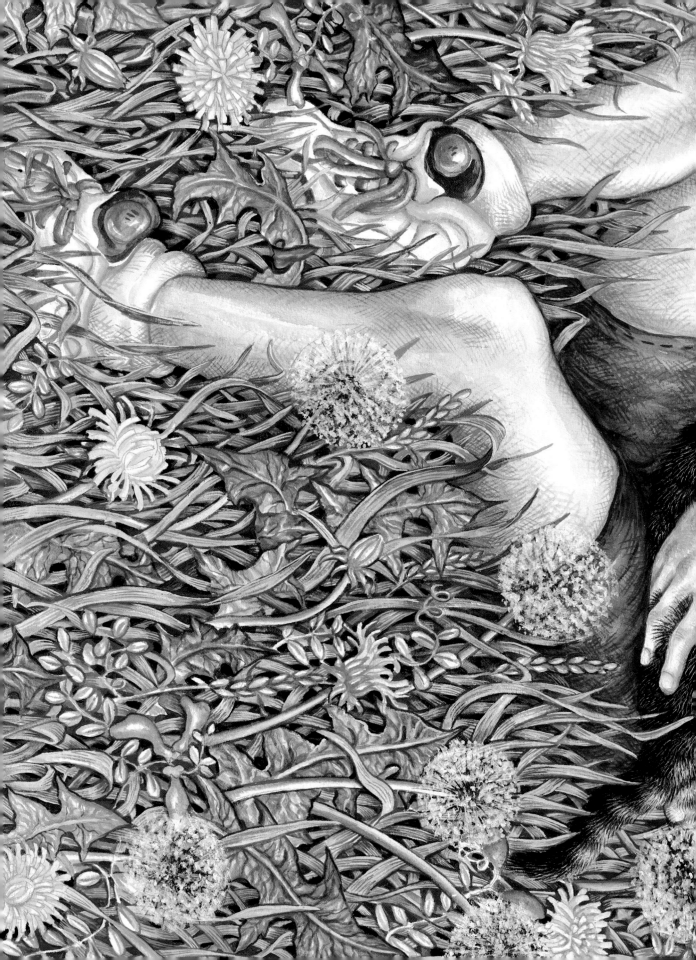

and came whiskers to nose with a funny creature.
It had two big green eyes and a furry head.
'Will you play with me?'

Turn the page and see who will play with Pumpkin.
Then *close* the book, turn it upside-down, and start
again *from the other end!*

Pumpkin crawled through the jungle of the grass

'Will you play with me?'
the kitten asked the birds.
'No,' sang the birds.
'We must find food to eat.'
And they flew off leaving only a feather behind.

'Will you play with me?'
Pumpkin asked the lady.
'Ouch, no!' she cried.
'I'm busy, go outside and play.'

'Will you play with me?'
'No,' yawned Captain, the old cat.
'I want to sleep and dream of fish.'

Pumpkin had a lovely home.
She had a warm soft bed and plenty of toys.
But she was lonely.
'Who will play with me?'

Who Will Play With Me?

Michele Coxon

Happy Cat Books